The New Minister's Great Opportunity, Saint Patrick, and The Village Convict

Heman White Chaplin

THE NEW MINISTER'S GREAT OPPORTUNITY.

By Heman White Chaplin

1887

First published in the "Century Magazine."

The New Minister's Great Opportunity

"The minister's got a job," said Mr. Snell.

Mr. Snell had been driven in by a shower from the painting of a barn, and was now sitting, with one bedaubed overall leg crossed over the other, in Mr. Hamblin's shop.

Half-a-dozen other men, who had likewise found in the rain a call to leisure, looked up at him inquiringly.

"How do you mean?" said Mr. Noyes, who sat beside him, girt with a nail-pocket. "'The minister 's got a job'? How do you mean?" And Mr. Noyes assumed a listener's air, and stroked his thin yellow beard.

Mr. Snell smiled, with half-shut, knowing eyes, but made no answer.

"How do you mean?" repeated Mr. Noyes; "'The minister's got a job' — of course he has — got a stiddy job. We knew that before."

"Very well," said Mr. Snell, with a placid face; "seeing's you know so much about it, enough said. Let it rest right there."

"But," said Mr. Noyes, nervously blowing his nose; "you lay down this proposition: 'The minister's got a job.' Now I ask, what is it?"

Mr. Snell uncrossed his legs, and stooped to pick up a last, which he proceeded to scan with a shrewd, critical eye.

"Narrer foot," he said to Mr. Hamblin.

"Private last — Dr. Hunter's," said Mr. Hamblin, laying down a boot upon which he was stitching an outer-sole, and rising to make a ponderous, elephantine excursion across the quaking shop to the earthen water-pitcher, from which he took a generous draught.

"Well, Brother Snell," said Mr. Noyes, — they were members together of a secret organization, of which Mr. Snell was P. G. W. T. F., —

"ain't you going to tell us? What—is this job? That is to say, what—er—is it?"

Brother Snell set his thumbs firmly in the armholes of his waistcoat, surveyed the smoke-stained pictures pasted on the wall, looked keen, and softly whistled.

At last he condescended to explain.

"Preaching Uncle Capen's funeral sermon."

There was a subdued general laugh. Even Mr. Hamblin's leathern apron shook.

Mr. Noyes, however, painfully looking down upon his beard to draw out a white hair, maintained his serious expression.

"I don't see much 'job' in that," he said; "a minister's supposed to preach a hundred and four sermons in each and every year, and there's plenty more where they come from. What's one sermon more or less, when stock costs nothing? It's like wheeling gravel from the pit."

"O.K.," said Mr. Snell; "if 't aint no trouble, then 't ain't But seeing's you know, suppose you specify the materials for this particular discourse."

Mr. Noyes looked a little disconcerted.

"Well," he said; "of course, I can't set here and compose a funereal discourse, off-hand, without no writing-desk; but there's stock enough to make a sermon of, any time."

"Oh, come," said Mr. Snell, "don't sneak out: particularize."

"Why," said Mr. Noyes, "you 've only to open the leds of your Bible, and choose a text, and then: When did this happen? Why did this happen? To who did this happen? and so forth and so on; and there's your sermon. I 've heard 'em so a hunderd times."

"All right," said Mr. Snell; "I don't doubt you know; but as for me, I for one never happened to hear of anything that Uncle Capen did

2

but whitewash and saw wood. Now what sort of an autobiographical sermon could you make out of sawing wood?"

Whereat Leander Buffum proceeded, by that harsh, guttural noise well known to country boys, to imitate the sound of sawing through a log. His sally was warmly greeted.

"The minister might narrate," said Mr. Blood, "what Uncle Capen said to Issachar, when Issachar told him that he charged high for sawing wood. 'See here,' says Uncle Capen, 's'pos'n I do. My arms are shorter'n other folks's, and it takes me just so much longer to do it.'"

"Well," said Mr. Noyes, "I'm a fair man; always do exactly right is the rule I go by; and I will frankly admit, now and here, that if it's a biographical discourse they want, they 'll have to cut corners."

"*Pre-cise-ly*" said Mr. Snell; "and that's just what they do want."

"Well, well," said Mr. Hamblin, laboriously rising and putting his spectacles into their silver case,—for it was supper-time,—"joking one side, if Uncle Capen never did set the pond afire, we 'd all rather take his chances to-day, I guess, than those of some smarter men."

At which Mr. Snell turned red; for he was a very smart man and had just failed,—to everybody's surprise, since there was no reason in the world why he should fail,—and had created more merriment for the public than joy among his creditors, by paying a cent and a half on the dollar.

"Come in; sit down," said Dr. Hunter, as the young minister appeared at his office door; and he tipped back in his chair, and put his feet upon a table. "What's the news?"

"Doctor," said Mr. Holt, laughing, as he laid down his hat and took an arm-chair; "you told me to come to you for any information. Now I want materials for a sermon on old Mr. Capen."

The Doctor looked at him with a half-amused expression, and then sending out a curl of blue smoke, he watched it as it rose melting into the general air.

3

"You don't smoke, I believe?" he said to the minister.

Holt smiled and shook his head.

The Doctor put his cigar back into his mouth, clasped one knee in his hands, and fixed his eyes in meditation on a one-eared Hippocrates looking down with a dirty face from the top of a bookcase. Perhaps the Doctor was thinking of the two or three hundred complimentary visits he had been permitted to make upon Uncle Capen within ten years.

Presently a smile broke over his face.

"I must tell you, before I forget it," he said, "how Uncle Capen nursed one of my patients. Years and years ago, I had John Ellis, our postmaster now, down with a fever. One night Uncle Capen watched—you know he was spry and active till he was ninety. Every hour he was to give Ellis a little ice-water; and when the first time came, he took a table-spoonful—there was only a dim light in the room—and poured the ice-water down Ellis's neck. Well, Ellis jumped, as much as so sick a man could, and then lifted his finger to his lips: 'Here 's my mouth,' said he. 'Why, why,' said Uncle Capen, 'is that your mouth? I took that for a wrinkle in your forehead."

The minister laughed.

"I have heard a score of such stories to-day," he said; "there seem to be enough of them; but I can't find anything adapted to a sermon, and yet they seem to expect a detailed biography."

"Ah, that's just the trouble," said the Doctor. "But let us go into the house; my wife remembers everything that ever happens, and she can post you up on Uncle Capen, if anybody can."

So they crossed the door-yard into the house.

Mrs. Hunter was sewing; a neighbor, come to tea, was crocheting wristers for her grandson.

They were both talking at once as the Doctor opened the sitting-room door.

"Since neither of you appears to be listening," he said, as they started up, "I shall not apologize for interrupting. Mr. Holt is collecting facts about Uncle Capen for his funeral sermon, and I thought that my good wife could help him out, if anybody could. So I will leave him."

And the Doctor, nodding, went into the hall for his coat and driving-gloves, and, going out, disappeared about the corner of the house.

"You will really oblige me very much, Mrs. Hunter," said the minister, "—or Mrs. French,—if you can give me any particulars about old Mr. Capen's life. His family seem to be rather sensitive, and they depend on a long, old-fashioned funeral sermon; and here I am utterly bare of facts."

"Why, yes," said Mrs. Hunter; "of course, now—"

"Why, yes; everybody knows all about him," said Mrs. French.

And then they laid their work down and relapsed into meditation.

"Oh!" said Mrs. Hunter, in a moment. "No, though—"

"Why, you know," said Mrs. French,—"no—I guess, on the whole"

"You remember," said the Doctor's wife to Mrs. French, with a faint smile, "the time he papered my east chamber—don't you—how he made the pattern come?"

And then they both laughed gently for a moment.

"Well, I have always known him," said Mrs. French. "But really, being asked so suddenly, it seems to drive everything out of my head."

"Yes," said Mrs. Hunter, "and it's odd that I can't think of exactly the thing, just at this min-ute; but if I do, I will run over to the parsonage this evening."

"Yes, so will I," said Mrs. French; "I know that I shall think of oceans of things just as soon as you are gone."

"Won't you stay to tea?" said Mrs. Hunter, as Holt rose to go. "The Doctor has gone; but we never count on him."

"No, I thank you," said Mr. Holt. "If I am to invent a biography, I may as well be at it."

Mrs. Hunter went with him to the door.

"I must just tell you," she said, "one of Uncle Capen's sayings. It was long ago, at the time I was married and first came here. I had a young men's Bible-class in Sunday-school, and Uncle Capen came into it. He always wore a cap, and sat at meetings with the boys. So, one Sunday, we had in the lesson that verse,—you know,—that if all these things should be written, even the world itself could not contain the books that should be written; and there Uncle Capen stopped me, and said he, 'I suppose that means the world as known to the ancients?'"

Holt put on his hat, and with a smile turned and went on his way toward the parsonage; but he remembered that he had promised to call at what the local paper termed "the late residence of the deceased," where, on the one hundredth birthday of the centenarian, according to the poet's corner,—

> "Friends, neighbors, and visitors he did receive
> From early in the morning till dewy eve."

So he turned his steps in that direction. He opened the clicking latch of the gate and rattled the knocker on the front door of the little cottage; and a tall, motherly woman of the neighborhood appeared and ushered him in.

Uncle Capen's unmarried daughter, a woman of sixty, her two brothers and their wives, and half-a-dozen neighbors were sitting in the tidy kitchen, where a crackling wood-fire in the stove was suggesting a hospitable cup of tea.

The ministers appearance, breaking the formal gloom, was welcomed.

"Well," said Miss Maria, "I suppose the sermon is all writ by this time. I think likely you 've come down to read it to us."

"No," said Holt, "I have left the actual writing of it till I get all my facts. I thought perhaps you might have thought of something else."

"No; I told you everything there was about father yesterday," she said. "I 'm sure you can't lack of things to put in; why, father lived a hundred years—and longer, too, for he was a hundred years and six days, you remember."

"You know," said Holt, "there are a great many things that are very interesting to a man's immediate friends that don't interest the public." And he looked to Mr. Small for confirmation.

"Yes, that 's so," said Mr. Small, nodding wisely.

"But, you see, father was a centenarian," said Maria, "and so that makes everything about him interesting. It's a lesson to the young, you know."

"Oh, yes, that's so," said Mr. Small, "if a man lives to be a centurion."

"Well, you all knew our good friend," said Mr. Holt. "If any of you will suggest anything, I shall be very glad to put it in."

Nobody spoke for a moment.

"There's one interesting thing," said one of the sons, a little old man much like his father; "that is, that none of his children have ever gone meandering off; we've all remained"—he might almost have said remained seated—"all our lives, right about him."

"I will allude to that," said Mr. Holt. "I hope you have something else, for I am afraid of running short of material: you see I am a stranger here."

"Why, I hope there won't be any trouble about it," said Maria, in sudden consternation. "I was a little afraid to give it out to so young a man as you, and I thought some of giving the preference to Father Cobb, but I did n't quite like to have it go out of the village, nor to deprive you of the opportunity; and they all assured me that you was smart. But if you 're feeling nervous, perhaps we 'd better have him still; he 's always ready."

"Just as you like," said Holt, modestly; "if he would be willing to preach the sermon, we might leave it that way, and I will add a few remarks." But Maria's zeal for Father Cobb was a flash in the pan. He was a sickly farmer, a licensed preacher, who, when he was called upon occasionally to meet a sudden exigency, usually preached on the beheading of John the Baptist.

"I guess you 've got things enough to write," said Maria, consolingly; "you know how awfully a thing doos drag out when you come to write it down on paper. Remember to tell how we 've all stayed right here."

When Holt went out, he saw Mr. Small beckoning him to come to where his green wagon stood under a tree.

"I must tell you," he said, with an awkwardly repressed smile, "about a trade of Uncle Capen's. He had a little lot up our way that they wanted for a schoolhouse, and he agreed to sell it for what it cost him, and the selectmen, knowing what it cost him,—fifty dollars,—agreed with him that way. But come to sign the deed, he called for a hundred dollars. 'How 's that,' says they; 'you bought it of Captain Sam Bowen for fifty dollars.' 'Yes, but see here,' says Uncle Capen, 'it's cost me on an average five dollars a year, for the ten year I 've had it, for manure and ploughing and seed, and that's fifty dollars more.' But you 've sold the garden stuff off it, and had the money,' says they. 'Yes,' says Uncle Capen, 'but that money 's spent and eat up long ago!'"

The minister smiled, shook hands with Mr. Small, and went home.

The church was crowded. Horses filled the sheds, horses were tied to the fences all up and down the street. Funerals are always popular in the country, and this one had a double element of attractiveness. The whole population of the town, having watched with a lively interest, for years back, Uncle Capen's progress to his hundredth birthday, expected now some electrical effect, analogous to an apotheosis.

In the front pews were the chief mourners, filled with the sweet intoxication of pre-eminence.

The opening exercises were finished, a hymn was sung, —

"Life is a span,"

and Father Cobb arose to make his introductory remarks.

He began with some reminiscences of the first time he saw Uncle Capen, some thirty years before, and spoke of having viewed him even then as an aged man, and of having remarked to him that he was walking down the valley of life with one foot in the grave. He called attention to Uncle Capen's virtues, and pointed out their connection with his longevity. He had not smoked for some forty years; therefore, if the youth who were present desired to attain his age, let them not smoke. He had been a total abstainer, moreover, from his seventieth year; let them, if they would rival his longevity, follow his example. The good man closed with a feeling allusion to the relatives, in the front pew, mourning like the disciples of John the Baptist after his "beheadment" Another hymn was sung, —

"A vapor brief and swiftly gone."

Then there was deep silence as the minister rose and gave out his text: *"I have been young, and now I am old."*

"At the time of the grand review in Washington," he said, "that mighty pageant that fittingly closed the drama of the war, I was a spectator, crippled then by a gun-shot wound, and unable to march. From an upper window I saw that host file by, about to record its greatest triumph by melting quietly into the general citizenship, — a mighty, resistless army about to fade and leave no trace, except here and there a one-armed man, or a blue flannel jacket behind a plough. Often now, when I close my eyes, that picture rises: that gallant host, those tattered flags; and I hear the shouts that rose when my brigade, with their flaming scarfs, went trooping by. Little as I may have done, as a humble member of that army, no earthly treasure could buy from me the thought of my fellowship with it, or even the memory of that great review.

"But that display was mere tinsel show compared with the great pageant that has moved before those few men who have lived through the whole length of the past hundred years.

"Before me lies the form of a man who, though he has passed his days with no distinction but that of an honest man, has lived through some of the most remarkable events of all the ages. For a hundred years a mighty pageant has been passing before him. I would rather have lived that hundred years than any other. I am deeply touched to reflect that he who lately inhabited this cold tenement of clay connects our generation with that of Washington. And it is impossible to speak of one whose great age draws together this assembly, without recalling events through which he lived.

"Our friend was born in this village. This town then included the adjoining towns to the north and south. The region was then more sparsely settled, although many houses standing then have disappeared. While he was sleeping peacefully in the cradle, while he was opening on the world childhood's wide, wondering eyes, those great men whose names are our perpetual benediction were planning for freedom from a foreign yoke. While he was passing through the happy years of early-childhood, the fierce clash of arms resounded through the little strip of territory which then made up the United States. I can hardly realize that, as a child, he heard as a fresh, new, real story, of the deeds of Lexington, from the lips of men then young who had been in the fight, or listened as one of an eager group gathered about the fireside, or in the old, now deserted tavern on the turnpike, to the story of Bunker Hill.

"And when, the yoke of tyranny thrown off, in our country and in France, Lafayette, the mere mention of whose name brings tears to the eyes of every true American, came to see the America that he loved and that loved him, he on whose cold, rigid face I now look down, joined in one of those enthusiastic throngs that made the visit like a Roman Triumph.

"But turn to the world of Nature, and think of the panoramic scenes that have passed before those now impassive eyes. In our friend's boyhood there was no practical mode of swift communication of news. In great emergencies, to be sure, some patriot hand might flash the beacon-light from a lofty tower; but news crept slowly over our hand-breath nation, and it was months after a presidential election before the result was generally known. He lived to see the

10

telegraph flashing swiftly about the globe, annihilating time and space and bringing the scattered nations into greater unity.

"And think, my hearers, for one moment, of the wonders of electricity. Here is a power which we name but do not know; which flashes through the sky, shatters great trees, burns buildings, strikes men dead in the fields; and we have learned to lead it, all unseen, from our house-tops to the earth; we tame this mighty, secret, unknown power into serving us as a a daily messenger; and no man sets the limits now to the servitude that we shall yet bind it down to.

"Again, my hearers, when our friend was well advanced in life, there was still no better mode of travel between distant points than the slow, rumbling stage-coach; many who are here remember well its delays and discomforts. He saw the first tentative efforts of that mighty factor steam to transport more swiftly. He saw the first railroad built in the country; he lived to see the land covered with the iron net-work.

"And what a transition is this! Pause for a moment to consider it. How much does this imply. With the late improvements in agricultural machinery, with the cheapening of steel rails, the boundless prairie farms of the West are now brought into competition with the fields of Great Britain in supplying the Englishman's table, and seem not unlikely, within this generation, to break down the aristocratic holding of land, and so perhaps to undermine aristocracy itself."

So the preacher continued, speaking of different improvements, and lastly of the invention of daguerreotypes and photographs. He called the attention of his hearers to this almost miraculous art of indelibly fixing the expression of a countenance, and drew a lesson as to the permanent effect of our daily looks and expression on those among whom we live. He considered at length the vast amount of happiness which had been caused by bringing pictures of loved ones within the reach of all; the increase of family affection and general good feeling which must have resulted from the invention; he suggested a possible change in the civilization of the older nations through the constant sending home, by prosperous adopted citizens, of photographs of themselves and of their homes, and alluded to the effect which this must have had upon immigration.

Finally he adverted to the fact that the sons of the deceased, who sat before him, had not yielded to the restless spirit of adventure, but had found "no place like home."

"But I fear," he said at last, "that the interest of my subject has made me transgress upon your patience; and with a word or two more I will close.

"When we remember what hard, trying things often arise within a single day, let us rightly estimate the patient well-doing of a man who has lived a blameless life for a hundred years. When we remember what harm, what sin, can be crowded into a single moment, let us rightly estimate the principle that kept him so close to the Golden Rule, not for a day, not for a decade or a generation, but for a hundred years.

"And now, as we are about to lay his deserted body in the earth, let not our perceptions be dulled by the constant repetition in this world of death and burial. At this hour our friend is no longer aged; wrinkles and furrows, trembling limbs and snowy locks he has left behind him, and he knows, we believe, to-day, more than the wisest philosopher on earth. We may study and argue, all our lives, to discover the nature of life, or the form it takes beyond the grave; but in one moment of swift transition the righteous man may learn it all. We differ widely one from another, here, in mental power. A slight hardening of some tissue of the brain might have left a Shakspeare an attorney's clerk. But, in the brighter world, no such impediments prevent, I believe, clear vision and clear expression; and differences of mind that seem world-wide here, may vanish there. When the spirit breaks its earthly prison and flies away, who can tell how bright and free the humblest of us may come to be! There may be a more varied truth than we commonly think, in the words, —'The last shall be first.'

"Let this day be remembered. Let us think of the vast display of Nature's forces which was made within the long period of our old neighbor's life; but let us also reflect upon the bright pageant that is now unrolling itself before him in a better world."

That evening Miss Maria and her brothers, sitting in state in the little old house, received many a caller; and the conversation was chiefly upon one theme,—not the funeral sermon, although that was commended as a frank and simple biographical discourse, but the great events which had accompanied Uncle Capen's progress through this world, almost like those which Horace records in his Ode to Augustus.

"That's trew, every word," said Apollos Carver; "when Uncle Capen was a boy there wasn't not one railroad in the hull breadth of the United States, and just think: why now you can go in a Pullerman car clear'n acrost to San Francisco. My daughter lives in Oakland, just acrost a ferry from there."

"Well, then, there 's photographing," said Captain Abel. "It doos seem amazing, as the minister said: you set down, and square yourself, and slick your hair, and stare stiddy into a funnel, and a man ducks his head under a covering, and pop! there you be, as natural as life,—if not more so. And when Uncle Capen was a young man, there wasn't nothing but portraits and minnytures, and these black-paper-and-scissors portraits,—what do they call 'em? Yes, sir, all that come in under his observation."

"Yes," said one of the sons, "'tis wonderful; my wife and me was took setting on a settee in the Garding of Eden,—lions and tigers and other scriptural objects in the background."

"And don't forget the telegrapht," said Maria; "don't forget that."

"Trew," said Apollos, "that's another thing. I hed a message come once-t from my son that lives to Taunton. We was all so sca't and faint when we see it, that we did n't none of us dast to open it, and finally the feller that druv over with it hed to open it fur us."

"What was there in it?" said Mr. Small; "sickness?—death?"

"No, he wanted his thick coat expressed up. But my wife didn't get over the shock for some time. Wonderful thing, that telegraph—

here's a man standing a hundred miles off, like enough, and harpooning an idea chock right into your mind."

"Then that was a beautiful truth," said Maria: "that father and Shakspeare would like enough be changed right round, in Heaven; I always said father wasn't appreciated here."

"Well," said Apollos, "'tis always so; we don't begin to realize the value of a thing tell we lose it. Now that we sort o' stand and gaze at Uncle Capen at a fair distance, as it were, he looms. Ef he only hed n't kep' so quiet, always, about them 'ere wonders. A man really ought, in justice to himself, to blow his own horn—jest a little. But that was a grand discourse, wa'n't it, now?"

"Oh, yes," said Maria, "though I did feel nervous for the young man. Still, when you come to think what materials he had to make a sermon out of,—why, how could he help it! And yet, I doubt not he takes all the credit to himself."

"I should really have liked to have heard Father Cobb treat the subject," said Mrs. Small, rising to go, and nodding to her husband. "'T was a grand theme. But 't was a real chance for the new minister. Such an opportunity doesn't happen not once in a lifetime."

The next morning, after breakfast, on his way home from the post-office, the minister stopped in at Dr. Hunter's office. The Doctor was reading a newspaper.

Mr. Holt took a chair in silence.

The Doctor laid down the paper and eyed him quizzically, and then slowly shook his head.

"I don't know about you ministers," he said. "I attended the funeral; I heard the biographical discourse; I understand it gave great satisfaction; I have reflected on it over night; and now, what I want to know is, what on earth 'there was in it about Uncle Capen."

The minister smiled.

"I think," he replied, "that all that I said about Uncle Capen was strictly true."

I.

One of the places which they point out on Ship Street is the Italian fruit-shop on the corner of Perry Court, before the door of which, six years ago, Guiseppe Cavagnaro, bursting suddenly forth in pursuit of Martin Lavezzo, stabbed him in the back, upon the sidewalk. "All two" of them were to blame, so the witnesses said; but Cavagnaro went to prison for fifteen years. That was the same length of time, as it happened, that the feud had lasted.

Nearly opposite is Sarah Ward's New Albion dance-hall. It opens directly from the street There is an orchestra of three pieces, one of which plays in tune. That calm and collected woman whom you may see rocking in the window, or sitting behind the bar, sewing or knitting, is not a city missionary, come to instruct the women about her; it is Sarah Ward, the proprietress. She knows the Bible from end to end. She was a Sunday-school teacher once; she had a class of girls; she spoke in prayer-meetings; she had a framed Scripture motto in her chamber, and she took the Teachers' Lesson Quarterly; she visited the sick; she prayed in secret for her scholars' conversion. How she came to change her views of life nobody knows, — that is to say, not everybody knows. And still she is honest. It is her pride that sailors are not drugged and robbed in the New Albion.

A few doors below, and on the same side of the street, is the dance-hall that was Bose King's-. It is here that pleasure takes on its most sordid aspect. If you wish to see how low a white woman can fall, how coarse and offensive a negro man can be, you will come here. There is an inscription on the bar, in conspicuous letters, — "Welcome Home."

By day it is comparatively still in Ship Street. Women with soulless faces loll stolidly in the open ground-floor windows. There are few customers in the bar-rooms; here and there two or three idlers shake for drinks. Policemen stroll listlessly about, and have little to do. But at nightfall there is a change; the scrape of fiddles, the stamp of boot-heels, is heard from the dance-halls. Oaths and boisterous laughter everywhere strike the ear. Children, half-clad, run loose at eleven o'clock. Two policemen at a corner interrogate a young man who is hot and excited and has no hat. He admits that he saw three men run from the alley-way and saw the sailor come staggering out after them, but he does not know who the men were. The policemen "take him in," on suspicion.

It is here that the Day-Star Mission has planted itself. Its white flag floats close by the spot where Martin Lavezzo fell, with the long knife between his shoulder-blades. Its sign of welcome is in close rivalry with the harsh strains from Sarah Ward's and the lighted stairway to Bose King's saloon. It stands here, isolated and strange, an unbidden guest. It is a protest, a reproof, a challenge, an uplifted finger.

But while, to a casual glance, the Day-Star Mission is all out of place, it has, nevertheless, its following. On Monday and Thursday afternoons a troop of black-eyed, jet-haired Portuguese women, half of whom are named Mary Jesus, flock in to a sewing-school. On Tuesdays and Fridays American, Scotch, and Irish women, from the tenement-houses of the quarter, fill the settees, to learn the use of the needle, to enjoy a little peace, and to hear reading and singing; and occasionally the general public of the vicinity are invited to an entertainment.

It was a February afternoon; at the Mission building the board were in monthly session. The meeting had been a spirited one. A proposition to amend the third line of the fourth by-law, entitled "Decorum in the Hall," by inserting the word "smoking," had been debated and had prevailed. A proposition to buy a new mangle for the laundry had been defeated, it having been humorously suggested that the women could mangle each other. Other matters of interest had been considered.

Finally, as the hour for adjournment drew near, a proposition was brought forth, appropriate to the season. Saint Patrick's Day was approaching. It was to many a day of temptation, particularly in the evening. Would it not be a good plan to hold out the helping hand, in the form of a Saint Patrick's Day festival, with an address, for example, upon Saint Patrick's life, with Irish songs and Irish readings? Such an entertainment would draw; it would keep a good many people out of the saloons. Such was the suggestion.

The proposition excited no little interest. Ladies who had begun to put on their wraps sat down again. To one of the board, a clergyman, who had lately been lecturing on "Popery the People's Peril," the proposition was startling. It looked toward the breaking down of all barriers; it gave Romanism an outright recognition. Another member, a produce-man, understood,—in fact he had read in his denominational weekly,—that Saint Patrick could be demonstrated to have been a Protestant, and he suggested that that fact might be "brought out." Others viewed the matter in that humorous light in which this festival day commonly strikes the American mind.

The motion prevailed. Even the anti-papistic clergyman was comforted, apparently, at last, for he was heard to whisper jocosely to his left-hand neighbor: "Saint Patrick's Day in the Morning!"

A committee, with the produce-man at the head, was appointed to select a speaker, and to provide music and reading. It was suggested that perhaps Mr. Wakeby and Mrs. Wilson-Smith would volunteer, if urged,—their previous charities in this direction had made them famous in the neighborhood. Mr. Wakeby to read from "Handy Andy;" Mrs. Wilson-Smith to sing "Kathleen Mavourneen,"—there would not be standing-room!

So finally unanimity prevailed, and with unanimity, enthusiasm.

The committee met, and the details were settled. The chairman quietly reserved to himself, by implication, the choice of a speaker. He knew that it would be an audience hard to hold. The occasion demanded a man of peculiar gifts. Such a man, he said to himself, he knew.

II.

The single meeting-house of L— — — stands on the main street, with its tall spire and its two tiers of gray-blinded windows. Beside it is the mossy burial-ground, where prim old ladies walk on Sunday afternoons, with sprigs of sweet-william.

Across the street, and a little way down the road, is the square white house with a hopper-roof, which an elderly, childless widow, departing this life some forty years ago, thoughtfully left behind her for a parsonage. It is a pleasant, home-like house, open to sun and air, and the pleasantest of all its rooms is the minister's study. It is an upper front chamber, with windows to the east and the south. There is nothing in the room of any value; but whether the minister is within, or is away and is represented only by his palm-leaf dressing-gown, somehow the spirit of peace seems always to abide there.

There is the ancient desk, which the minister's children, when they were little, used to call the "omnibus," by reason of a certain vast and capacious drawer, the resort of all homeless things,—nails, wafers, the bed-key, curtain-fixtures, carpet-tacks, and dried rhubarb. Perhaps it was to this drawer that the minister's daughter lately referred, when she said that the true motto was, "One place for everything, and everything in that one place."

Over the chimney-piece hangs a great missionary map, showing the stations of the different societies, with a key at one side. This blue square in Persia denotes a missionary post of the American Board of Commissioners; that red cross in India is an outpost of a Presbyterian missionary society; this green diamond in Arrapatam marks a station of the Free Church Missionary Union. As one looks the map over, he seems to behold the whole missionary force at work. He sees, in imagination, Mr. Elmer Small, from Augusta, Maine, preaching predestination to a company of Karens, in a house of reeds, and the Rev. Geo. T. Wood, from Massachusetts, teaching Paley in Roberts College at Constantinople.

Thus the whole Christian world lies open before you.

Pinned up on one of the doors is the Pauline Chart. Have you never seen the Pauline Chart? It was prepared in colored inks, by Mr. Parker, a theological student with a turn for penmanship, and lithographed, and was sold by him to eke out the avails of what are inaptly termed "supplies." You would find it exceedingly convenient. It shows in a tabulated form, for ready reference, the incidents of Saint Paul's career, arranged chronologically. Thus you can find at a glance the visit to Berea, the stoning at Lystra, or the tumult at Ephesus. Its usefulness is obvious. Over the desk is a map of the Holy Land, with mountain elevations.

The walls of the room are for the most part hidden by books. The shelves are simple affairs of stained maple, covered heavily with successive coats of varnish, cracked, as is that of the desk, by age and heat. The contents are varied. Of religious works there are the Septuagint, in two fat little blue volumes, like Roman candles; Conant's Genesis; Hodge on Romans; Hackett on Acts, which the minister's small children used to spell out as "Jacket on Acts;" Knott on the Fallacies of the Antinomians; A Tour in Syria; Dr. Grant and the Mountain Nestorians, and six Hebrew Lexicons, singed by fire, — a paternal inheritance.

There are a good many works, too, of general literature, but rather oddly selected, as will happen where one makes up his library chiefly by writing book-notices: Peter Bayne's Essays; Coleridge; the first volume of Masson's Life of Milton; Vanity Fair; the Dutch Republic; the Plurality of Worlds; and Mommsen's Rome. That very attractive book in red you need not take down; it is only the history of Norwalk, Conn., with the residence of J. T. Wales, Esq., for a frontispiece; the cover is all there is to it. Finally, there are two shelves of Patent Office Reports, and Perry's Expedition to Japan with a panoramic view of Yeddo. This shows that the minister has numbered a congressman among his flock.

It is here that Dr. Parsons is diligently engaged, this cold March afternoon, to the music of his crackling air-tight stove. He is deeply absorbed in his task, and we may peep in and not disturb him. He has a large number of books spread out before him; but looking them over, we miss Lange's Commentaries, Bengel's Gnomon, Cobb on Galatians,—those safe and sound authorities always provided with the correct view.

The books which lie before the Doctor seem all to, deal with a Romish Saint, and, of all the saints in the world, Saint Patrick. In full sight of his own steeple, from which the bell is even now counting out the sixty-nine years of a good brother just passed away in hope of a Protestant heaven,—tolling out the years for the village housewives, who pause and count; under such hallowing influences,—beneath, as it were, the very shadow of the Missionary Map and the Pauline Chart, and with a gray Jordan rushing down through a scarlet Palestine directly before him, suggestive of all good things; with Knott on the Fallacies at his right hand, and with Dowling on Romanism on his left, the Doctor is actually absorbed in Papistical literature. Here are the works of Dr. Lanigan and Father Colgan and Monseigneur Moran. Here is the "Life and Legends of Saint Patrick," illustrated, with a portrait in gilt of Brian Boru on the cover. Here are the Tripartite Life, in Latin, and the saint's Confession, and the Epistle to Co-roticus, the Ossianic Poems, and Miss Cusack's magnificent quarto, which the Doctor has borrowed from the friendly priest at the factory village four miles away, who borrowed it from the library of the Bishop to lend to him.

Perhaps you have never undertaken to prepare a life of Saint Patrick. If so, you have no idea of the difficulties of the task. In the first place, you must settle the question whether Saint Patrick ever existed. And this is a disputed point; for while there are those, like Father Colgan, whose clear faith accepts Saint Patrick just as he stands in history and tradition, yet, on the other hand, there are sceptics, like Ledwick, who contend that the saint is nothing but a prehistoric myth, floating about in the imagination of the Irish people.

Having settled to your satisfaction that Patrick really lived, you must next proceed to fix the date of his birth; and here you enter upon complicated calculations. You will probably decide to settle first, as a starting-point, the date of the saint's escape from captivity; and to do this you will have to reconcile the fact that after the captivity he paid a friendly visit to his kinsman, Saint Martin of Tours, who died in 397, with the fact that he was not captured until 400.

Next you will come to the matter of the saint's birthplace; and this is a delicate question, for you will have to decide between the claims of Ireland, of Scotland, and of France; and you will very probably find yourself finally driven to the conclusion—for the evidence points that way—that Saint Patrick was a Frenchman.

Next comes the question of the saint's length of days; and if you attempt to include only the incidents of his life of which there can be no possible doubt, you will stretch his age on until you will probably fix it at one hundred and twenty years.

But when you have settled the existence, the date of birth, and the nationality of Saint Pat-rick, you are still only upon the threshold of your inquiries; for you next find before you for examination a vast variety of miracles, accredited to him, which you must examine, weeding out such as are puerile and are manifestly not well established, and retaining such as are proved to your satisfaction. You will be struck at once with the novel and interesting character of some of them. Prince Caradoc was changed into a wolf. An Irish magician who opposed the saint was swallowed by the earth as far as his ears, and then, on repentance, was instantly cast forth and set free. An Irish pagan, dead and long buried, talked freely with the saint from out his turf-covered grave, and charitably explained where a certain cross belonged which had been set by mistake over him. The saint was captured once, and was exchanged for a kettle, which thenceforth froze water over the fire instead of boiling it, until the saint was sent back and the kettle returned. Ruain, son of Cucnamha, Amhalgaidh's charioteer, was blind. He went in haste to meet Saint Patrick, to be healed. Mignag laughed at him. "My troth," said Patrick, "it would be fit that you were the blind one." The blind man was healed and the seeing one was made blind; Roi-Ruain is the name of the place where this was done. Patrick's charioteer was looking for his horses in the dark, and could not find them; Patrick lifted up his hand; his five fingers illuminated the place like five torches, and the horses were found.

You see that one has a good deal to go through who undertakes to prepare a life of Saint Patrick.

But our thoughts have wandered from Dr. Parsons. He has gathered the books before him with great pains, from public and private libraries, and he religiously meant to make an exhaustive study of them all; but sermons and parish calls and funerals, and that little affair of Mrs. Samuel Nute, have forced him, by a process of which we all know something, to forego his projected subsoil ploughing and make such hasty preparation as he can.

He has read the Confession and the Epistle to Coroticus, and he has glanced over the "Life and Legends," reading in a cursory way of the leper's miraculous voyage; of the fantastic snow; of the tombstone that sailed the seas; of the two trout that Patrick left to live forever in a well, —

> *"The two inseparable trout,*
> *Which would advance against perpetual streams,*
> *Without obligation, without transgression —*
> *Angels will be along with them in it."*

And being very fond of pure water himself, the Doctor is touched by Patrick's lament when far away from the well Uaran-gar: —

> *"Uaran-gar, Uaran-gar!*
> *O well, which I have loved, which loved me!*
> *Alas! my cry, O my dear God,*
> *That my drink is not from the pure well of Uaran-gar!"*

But finally he has settled down, as most casual students will, to the sincere and charming little sketch by William Bullen Morris, — "Saint Patrick, the Apostle of Ireland." He is reading it now by the east window, holding the book at arm's-length, as is his wont.

The theme is new to him. There opens up a fresh and interesting field. The dedication of the little book strikes his imagination: "To the Members of the Confraternity of Saint Patrick, established at the London Oratory, who, with the children of the saint in many lands, are the enduring witnesses of the faith which seeth Him who is invisible."

He is interested in the motto on the title-page, —*"En un mot, on y voit beaucoup le caractère de S. Paul,"* and in the authorization, —*"Nihil obstat*. E. S. Keagh, Cong. Orat." "*Imprimatur*, + Henricus Eduardus, Card."

The Doctor looks through the book in order. First, the introduction; and here he considers the questions—First, was there in fact such a man as Saint Patrick? Second, what was his nationality? Third, when was he born: and, herein, does the date of his escape from captivity conflict with the date of his visit to his kinsman, Saint Martin of Tours? Fourth, to what age did he live? Fifth, where and by whom was he converted? Sixth, are his miracles authentic? and so forth.

After this introductory study the book takes up the saint's life in connected order. Patrick was the son of a Roman decurio. From his earliest days wonders attended him. When he was an infant, and was about to be baptized, it happened that no water was to be had for the sacrament; whereupon, at the sign of the cross, made by the priest with the infant's hand upon the earth, a fountain gushed forth from the ground, and the priest, who was blind, anointing his own eyes with the water, received his sight.

As Patrick grew older, wonders multiplied. He came as an apostle of the faith to Strangford Lough. Dichu, the prince of that province, forewarned by the Druids, raised his sword at Patrick; but instantly his hand was fixed in the air, as if carved of stone; then light came to Dichu's soul, and from a foe he became a loving disciple.

Then comes the story of the fast upon the mountain. It was on the height ever since called Cruachan Patrick, which looks to the north upon Clew Bay, and to the west on the waters of the Atlantic. It was Shrove Saturday, a year and a little more from the apostle's first landing in Ireland. Already he had carried the gospel from the eastern to the western sea. But his spirit longed for the souls of the whole Irish nation. Upon the mountain he knelt in prayer, and as he prayed, his faith and his demands assumed gigantic proportions. An angel came down and addressed him. God could not grant his requests, the message ran, they were too great. "Is that his decision?" asked Patrick. "It is," said the angel. "It may be his," said Patrick, "it is not mine; for my decision is not to leave this cruachan until my demands are granted."

The angel departed. For forty days and forty nights Patrick fasted and prayed amid sore temptations. The blessing must fall upon all his poor people of Erin. As he prayed, he wept, and his cowl was drenched with his tears.

At last the angel returned and proposed a compromise. The vast Atlantic lay before them. Patrick might have as many souls as would cover its expanse as far as his eyes could reach. But he was not satisfied with that; his eyes, he said, could not reach very far over those heaving waters; he must have, in addition, a multitude vast enough to cover the land that lay between him and the sea. The angel yielded, and now bade him leave the mountain. But Patrick would not. "I have been tormented," he said, "and I must be gratified; and unless my prayers are granted I will not leave this cruachan while I live; and after my death there shall be here a caretaker for me."

The angel departed. Patrick went to his offering.

At evening the angel returned. "How am I answered?" asked Patrick. "Thus," said the angel: "all creatures, visible and invisible, including the Twelve Apostles, have entreated for thee,—and they have obtained. Strike thy bell and fall upon thy knees: for the blessing shall be on all Erin, both living and dead." "A blessing on the bountiful King that hath given," said Patrick; "now will I leave the cruachan."

It was on Holy Thursday that he came down from the mountain and returned to his people.

III.

One afternoon at about this time you might have seen Mr. Cole, the missionary of the Day-Star,—a small, lithe man, with a red beard,—making his way up town. He walked rapidly, as he always did, for he was a busy man.

He was an exceedingly busy man. During the past year, as was shown by his printed report, he had made 2,014 calls, or five and one-half calls a day; he had read the Scriptures in families 792 times; he had distributed 931,456 pages of religious literature; he had conversed on religious topics with 3,918 persons, or ten and seven-tenths persons per day, Sabbaths included. It was perhaps because he was so busy that there was complaint sometimes that he mixed matters and took things upon his shoulders which belonged to others.

Mr. Cole's rapid pace soon brought him to a broad and pleasant cross-street; he went up the high steps of one of the houses, rang the bell, and was admitted.

Rev. Mr. Martin was in his study, and the missionary was shown up. Precisely what the conversation was has not been reported; but certain it is that the next day after Mr. Cole's call, Mr. Martin began to prepare himself for an address upon the life of Saint Patrick. It was an entirely new topic to him; but he soon found himself in the full current of the stream, considering—First, did such a man really exist, or is Saint Patrick a mere myth, floating in the imagination of the Irish people? Second, what was his nationality? Third, where was he born, and, herein, how are we to reconcile his escape from captivity in 493, with his visit to his kinsman, Saint Martin of Tours, after his escape from captivity, in 490? Fourth, to what age did he live? Fifth,—and so forth.

Mr. Martin had begun his labors by taking down his encyclopaedia and such books of reference as he had thought could help him, and had succeeded so far as to get an outline of the saint's life, and to find mention of several works which treated of this topic. There were

Montalembert's "Monks of the West," and Dr. O'Donovan's "Annals of the Four Masters," the works of Monseigneur Moran and Father Colgan, the Tripartite Life, and a certain "magnificent quarto" by Miss Cusack. All these and many more he had hoped to find in the different libraries of the city. But great had been his surprise, on visiting the libraries, to find that the books he wanted were invariably out. It was a little startling, at first, to come upon this footprint in the sand; but a little reflection set the feeling at rest. The subject was an odd one to him, to be sure, but there were thousands of people in the city who might very naturally be concerned in it, particularly at this time, when Saint Patrick's Day was approaching. None the less the fact remained that the books he wanted—scattered through two or three libraries—were always out.

As he stepped out from the Free Library into the street, it occurred to him to go to a Catholic bookstore near at hand to look for what he wanted.

It was a large, showy shop, with Virgins and crucifixes and altar candelabra's in the windows, and pictures of bleeding hearts. He went in and stood at the counter. A rosy-faced servant-girl, with a shy, pleased expression, was making choice of a rosary. A young priest, a few steps away, was looking at an image of Saint Joseph.

The salesman left the servant-girl to her hesitating choice, and turned to Mr. Martin.

"What have you," asked Mr. Martin, with a slightly conscious tone, "upon the life of Saint Patrick?"

The priest turned and looked; but the salesman, with an unmoved countenance, went to the shelves and selected two volumes and laid them in silence on the counter. One was the "Life and Legends of Saint Patrick" with a picture in gilt of Brian Boru on the cover. The other was "Saint Patrick, the Apostle of Ireland," by William Bullen Morris, Priest of the Oratory. They were both green-covered.

Early in the evening Mr. Martin settled down by his study fire to his new purchases. First he took up the "Life and Legends." He read the saint's own Confession, and the Letter to Co-roticus, and looked through the translation of the Tripartite Life, with its queer mixture of Latin and English: "Prima feria venit Patricius ad Talleriam, where the regal assembly was, to Cairpre, the son of Niall." "Interrogat autem Patricius qua causa venit Conall, and Conall related the reason to Patrick."

He glanced over the miracles and wonders of which this book was full. But before very long he laid it aside and took up the Life by William Bullen Morris, Priest of the Oratory, and decided that he must depend upon that for his preparation.

It was late at night. It was full time to stop reading; but it laid strong hold of his imagination, — this strange, intense, and humorous figure, looming up all new to him from the mists of the past. He read the book to the end; he read how the good Saint Bridget foretold the apostle's death; how two provinces contended for his remains, and how a light shone over his burial-place after he was laid to rest.

It was very late when Mr. Martin finished the book and laid it down.

Thus it happens that the Rev. Dr. Parsons and the Rev. Mr. Martin are both preparing themselves at the same time on the life of Saint Patrick, from this one brief book by William Bullen Morris, Priest of the Oratory.

IV.

Saint Patrick's Day has come and is now fast waning. The sun has sunk behind the chimney-stack of the New Albion dance-hall; the street lamps are lighted and are faintly contending against the dull glow of the late afternoon.

There is a lull between day and evening. All day there has been a stir in the city. There has been a procession in green sashes, with harps on the banners,—a long procession, in barouches, on horseback, and afoot. There have been impassioned addresses before the Hibernian Society and the Saint Peter's Young Men's Irish Catholic Benevolent Association. There has been more or less celebration in Ship Street.

The evening advances. It is seven o'clock. Strains of invitation issue from all the dance-halls. Already the people have begun to file in to the Day-Star Mission. The audience-room is on the street floor. The missionary stands at the open door, with anxious smiles, urging decorum. A knot of idlers on each side of the doorway, on the sidewalk, comment freely on him and on those who enter. Every moment or two a policeman forces them back.

At a quarter of seven a preliminary praise-meeting begins. Singing from within jars against the fiddling from over the way. You hear at once "Come to Jesus just now!" and "Old Dan Tucker."

Already the seats are filled,—eight in a settee; those who come now will have to stand. Still, people continue to file in: laborers, Portuguese sewing-women, two or three firemen in long-tailed coats and silver buttons, from Hook and Ladder Six, in the next block; gross-looking women, *habitués* of the Mission, with children; women who are *habitués* of no mission; prosperous saloon-keepers; one of the councilmen of the ward,—he is a saloon-keeper too.

Dr. Parsons's train brought him to town in good season. He passed in with other invited guests at the private door, and he has been upon the platform for ten minutes. His daughter is beside him; ten or a dozen of his parishioners, who have come too, occupy seats directly in front.

The platform seats are nearly all taken; it is time to begin. The street-door opens and a passage is made for a new-comer. It is Mr. Martin. A contingent from his church come with him and fill the few chairs that are still reserved about the desk.

Now all would appear to be ready; but there is still a few moments' pause. The missionary is probably completing some preliminary arrangements. The audience sit in stolid expectation.

Dr. Parsons, from beneath his eyebrows, is studying the faces before him. In this short time his address has entirely changed form in his mind. It was simple as he had planned it; it must be simpler yet But he has felt the pulse of the people before him. He feels that he can hold them, that he can stir them.

Meanwhile a whispered colloquy is going on, at the rear of the platform, between the missionary and the chairman of the committee for the evening. The missionary appears to be explanatory and apologetic, the chairman flushed. In a moment a hand is placed on Dr. Parsons's shoulder. He starts, half rises, and turns abruptly.

There has been, it seems, an unfortunate misunderstanding. Through some mistake Mr. Martin has been asked to make the address upon the life of Saint Patrick, and has prepared himself with care. He is one of the Mission's most influential friends; his church is among its chief benefactors. It is an exceedingly painful affair; but will Dr. Parsons give way to Mr. Martin?

So it is all over. The Doctor takes his seat and looks out again upon those hard, dreary faces,—his no longer. He has not realized until now how he has been looking forward to this evening. But the vision has fled. No ripples of uncouth laughter, no ready tears. No reaching these dull, violated hearts through the Saint whom they adore: that privilege is another's.

But the chairman again draws near. Will Dr. Parsons make the opening prayer?

The Doctor bows assent. He folds his arms and closes his eyes. You can see that he is trying to concentrate his thoughts in preparation for prayer. It is doubtless hard to divert them from the swift channel in which they have been bounding along.

Now all is ready. The missionary touches a bell, the signal for silence.

The Doctor rises. For a moment he stands looking over the rows on rows of hardened faces,—looking on those whom he has so longed to reach. He raises his hand; there is a dead silence, and he begins.

It was inevitable, at the outset, that he should refer to the occasion which had brought us together. It was natural to recall that we were come to celebrate the birth of an uncommon man. It was natural to suggest that he was no creature of story or ancient legend, floating about in the imagination of an ignorant people, but a real man like us, of flesh and blood. It was natural to add that he was a man born centuries ago; that the scene of his labors was the green island across the sea, where many of us now present had first seen the light. It was natural to give thanks for that godly life which had led three nations to claim the good man's birthplace. It was natural to suggest that if about the sweet memories of this man's life fancy had fondly woven countless legends, we might, with a discerning eye, read in them all the saintly power of the man of God. What though his infant hand may not have caused earthly waters to gush from the ground and heal the blindness of the ministering priest, nevertheless doth childhood ever call forth a well-spring of life, giving fresh sight to the blind,—to teacher and taught.

But why go on? Who has not heard, again and again, the old-fashioned prayer wherein all is laid forth, in outline, but with distinctness! We give thanks for this. May this be impressed upon our hearts. May this lead us solemnly to reflect.

The heart that is full must overflow,—if not in one way, then in another.

Mr. Martin has not been told about Dr. Parsons. He sits and listens as the Doctor goes on in the innocence of his heart, pouring forth with warmth and fervor the life of the saint according to William Bullen Morris, Priest of the Oratory,—pouring forth in unmistakable detail Mr. Martin's projected discourse.

The prayer is ended; a hymn is sung, and then the missionary presents to the audience the Rev. Mr. Martin, whom they are always delighted to hear; he will now address them upon the life of Saint Patrick.

Mr. Martin rises. He takes a sip of water. He coughs slightly. He passes his handkerchief across his lips. So far all is well. But the prayer is in his mind. Moreover, he unfortunately catches his wife's eye, with a suggestion of suppressed merriment in it.

What does he say? What can he say? There are certain vague lessons from the saint's virtues; some applications of what the Doctor has set forth; that is all. Saint Patrick was sober; we should be sober. Saint Patrick was kind; we should be kind.

Even his own parishioners admitted that he had not been "happy" on this particular occasion.

But at the close of the meeting Dr. Parsons received a compliment. As he descended from the platform, Mr. John Keenan, who kept the best-appointed bar-room on the street, advanced to meet him. Mr. Keenan was in an exceedingly happy frame of mind. He grasped the Doctor's hand. "I wish, sir," he said, with a fine brogue, "to congratulate you upon your very eloquent prayer. It remind me, sir,—and I take pleasure to say it,—it remind me, sir, of the Honorable John Kelly's noble oration on Daniel O'Connell."

Late that evening the Doctor stood at his study-window, looking out for a moment before retiring to rest. There was no light in the room, and the maps and the charts and the tall book-shelves were only outlines. There was a glimmer from a farm-house two miles away, where they were watching with the dead.

The Doctor's daughter came in with a light in her hand to bid her father good-night.

"What did you think, Pauline," he said to her, "of Mr. Martin's talk?" It had not been mentioned till now.

Pauline hardly knew what to think. She knew that it was not what the Rev. Dr. Parsons would have given them! But, honestly, what did her father think of it?

The Doctor mused for a moment; then he gave his judgment. "I think," he said, "that it showed a certain lack of preparation."

THE VILLAGE CONVICT

By Heman White Chaplin

1887

First published in the "Century Magazine."

The Village Convict

"Wonder 'f Eph's got back; they say his sentence run out yisterday."

The speaker, John Doane, was a sunburnt fisherman, one of a circle of well-salted individuals who sat, some on chairs, some on boxes and barrels, around the stove in a country store.

"Yes," said Captain Seth, a middle-aged little man with ear-rings; "he come on the stage to-noon. Would n't hardly speak a word, Jim says. Looked kind o' sot and sober."

"Wall," said the first speaker, "I only hope he won't go to burnin' us out of house and home, same as he burnt up Eliphalet's barn. I was ruther in hopes he 'd 'a' made off West. Seems to me I should, in his place, hevin' ben in State's-prison."

"Now, I allers hed quite a parcel o' sympathy for Eph," said a short, thickset coasting captain, who sat tilted back in a three-legged chair, smoking lazily. "You see, he wa'n't but about twenty-one or two then, and he was allers a mighty high-strung boy; and then Eliphalet did act putty ha'sh, foreclosin' on Eph's mother, and turnin' her out o' the farm in winter, when everybody knew she could ha' pulled through by waitin.' Eph sot great store by the old lady, and I expect he was putty mad with Eliphalet that night."

"I allers," said Doane, "approved o' his plan o' leadin' out all the critters, 'fore he touched off the barn. 'T ain't everybody 't would hev taken pains to do that. But all the same, I tell Sarai 't I feel kind o' skittish, nights, to hev to turn in, feelin' 't there's a convict in the place."

"I hain't got no barn to burn," said Captain Seth; "but if he allots my hen-house to the flames, I hope he'll lead out the hens and hitch 'em to the apple-trees, same's he did Eliphalet's critters. Think he ought to deal ekally by all."

34

A mild general chuckle greeted this sally, cheered by which the speaker added, —

"Thought some o' takin' out a policy o' insurance on my cockerel."

"Trade's lookin' up, William," said Captain Seth to the storekeeper, as some one was heard to kick the snow off his boots on the door-step. "Somebody 's found he's got to hev a shoestring 'fore mornin'."

The door opened, and closed behind a strongly-made man of twenty-six or seven, of homely features, with black hair, in clothes which he had outgrown. It was a bitter night, but he had no coat over his flannel jacket. He walked straight down the store, between the dry-goods counters, to the snug corner at the rear, where the knot of talkers sat; nodded, without a smile, to each of them, and then asked the storekeeper for some simple articles of food, which he wished to buy. It was Eph.

While the purchases were being put up, an awkward silence prevailed, which the oil-suits hanging on the walls, broadly displaying their arms and legs, seemed to mock, in dumb show.

Nothing was changed, to Eph's eyes, as he looked about. Even the handbill of familiar pattern —

"STANDING WOOD FOR SALE.
Apply to J. CARTER, Admin'r,"

seemed to have always been there.

The village parliament remained spellbound. Mr. Adams tied up the purchases, and mildly inquired, —

"Shall I charge this?"

Not that he was anxious to open an account, but that he would probably have gone to the length of selling Eph a barrel of molasses "on tick" rather than run any risk of offending so formidable a character.

"No," said Eph; "I will pay for the things."

And having put the packages into a canvas bag, and selected some fish-hooks and lines from the show-case, where they lay environed by jack-knives, jews-harps, and gum-drops,—dear to the eyes of childhood,—he paid what was due, said "Good-night, William," to the storekeeper, and walked steadily out into the night.

"Wall," said the skipper, "I am surprised! I strove to think o' suthin' to say, all the time he was here, but I swow I couldn't think o' nothin'. I could n't ask him if it seemed good to git home, nor how the thermometer had varied in different parts o' the town where he 'd been. Everything seemed to fetch right up standin' to the State's-prison."

"I was just goin' to say, 'How'd ye leave everybody?'" said Doane; "but that kind o' seemed to bring up them he 'd left. I felt real bad, though, to hev the feller go off 'thout none on us speakin' to him. He 's got a hard furrer to plough; and yet I don't s'pose there 's much harm in him, 'f Eliphalet only keeps quiet."

"Eliphalet!" said a young sailor, contemptuously. "No fear o' him! They say he 's so sca't of Eph he hain't hardly swallowed nothin' for a week."

"But where will he live?" asked a short, curly-haired young man, whom Eph had seemed not to recognize. It was the new doctor, who, after having made his way through college and the great medical school in Boston, had, two years before, settled in this village.

"I believe," said Mr. Adams, rubbing his hands, "that he wrote to Joshua Carr last winter, when his mother died, not to let the little place she left, on the Salt Hay Road; and I understand that he is going to make his home there. It is an old house, you know, and not worth much, but it is weather-tight, I should say."

"Speakin' of his writin' to Joshua," said Doane, "I have heard such a sound as that he used to shine up to Joshua's Susan, years back. But that 's all ended now. You won't catch Susan marryin' no jailbirds."

"But how will he live?" said the doctor. "Will anybody give him work?"

"Let him alone for livin'," said Doane. "He can ketch more fish than any other two men in the place—allers seemed to kind o' hev a knack o' whistlin' 'em right into the boat. And then Nelson Briggs, that settled up his mother's estate, allows he 's got over a hundred and ten dollars for him, after payin' debts and all probate expenses. That and the place is all he needs to start on."

"I will go to see him," said the doctor to himself, as he went out upon the requisition of a grave man in a red tippet, who had just come for him. "He does n't look so very dangerous, and I think he can be tamed. I remember that his mother told me about him."

Late that night, returning from his seven miles' drive, as he left the causeway, built across a wide stretch of salt-marsh, crossed the rattling plank bridge, and ascended the hill, he saw a light in the cottage window, where he had often been to attend Aunt Lois. "I will stop now," said he. And, tying his horse to the front fence, he went toward the kitchen door. As he passed the window, he glanced in. A lamp was burning on the table. On a settle, lying upon his face, was stretched the convict, his arms beneath his head. The canvas bag lay on the floor beside him. "I will not disturb him now," said the doctor.

A few days later Dr. Burt was driving in his sleigh with his wife along the Salt Hay Road. It was a clear, crisp winter forenoon. As they neared Eph's house, he said,—

"Mary, suppose I lay siege to the fort this morning. I see a curl of smoke rising from the little shop in the barn. He must be making himself a jimmy or a dark-lantern to break into our vegetable cellar with."

"Well," said she, "I think it would be a good plan; only, you know, you must be very, very careful not to hint, even in the faintest way, at his imprisonment. You mustn't so much as *suspect* that he has ever been away from the place. People hardly dare to speak to him, for fear he will see some reference to his having been in prison, and get angry."

"You shall see my sly tact," said her husband, laughing. "I will be as innocent as a lamb. I will ask him why I have not seen him at the Sabbath-school this winter."

"You may make fun," said she, "but you will end by taking my advice, all the same. Now, do be careful what you say."

"I will," he replied. "I will compose my remarks carefully upon the back of an envelope and read them to him, so as to be absolutely sure. I will leave on his mind an impression that I have been in prison, and that he was the judge that tried me."

He drove in at the open gate, hitched his horse in a warm corner by the kitchen door, and then stopped for a moment to enjoy the view. The situation of the little house, half a mile from any other, was beautiful in summer, but it was bleak enough in winter. In the small front dooryard stood three lofty, wind-blown poplars, all heading away from the sea, and between them you could look down the bay or across the salt-marshes, while in the opposite direction were to be seen the roofs and the glittering spires of the village.

"It is social for him here, to say the least," said the doctor, as he turned and walked alone to the shop. He opened the door and went in. It was a long, low lean-to, such as farmers often furnish for domestic work with a carpenter's bench, a grindstone, and a few simple tools. It was lighted by three square windows above the bench. An air-tight stove, projecting its funnel through a hole in one of the panes, gave out a cheerful crackling.

Eph, in his shirt-sleeves, his hands in his pockets, was standing, his back against the bench, surveying, with something of a mechanic's eye, the frame of a boat which was set up on the floor.

He looked up and colored slightly. The doctor took out a cigarette, lit it, sat down on the bench, and smoked, clasping one knee in his hands and eying the boat.

"Centre-board?" he asked, at length.

"Yes," said Eph.

"Cat-rig?"

"Yes."

"Going fishing?"

"Yes."

"Alone?"

"Yes."

"I was brought up to sail a boat," said the doctor, "and I go fishing in summer—when I get a chance. I shall try your boat, some time."

No reply.

"The timbers aren't seasoned, are they? They look like pitch-pine, just out of the woods. Won't they warp?"

"No. Pitch-pine goes right in, green. I s'pose the pitch keeps it, if it's out of the sun."

"Where did you cut it?"

Eph colored a little.

"In my back lot."

The doctor smoked on calmly, and studied the boat.

"I don't know as I know you," said Eph, relaxing a little.

"Good reason," said the doctor. "I 've only been here two years;" and after a moment's pause, he added: "I am the doctor here, now. You 've heard of my father, Dr. Burt, of Broad River?"

Eph nodded assent; everybody knew him, all through the country,— a fatherly old man, who rode on long journeys at everybody's call, and never sent in his bills.

The visitor had a standing with Eph at once.

"Doctors never pick at folks," he said to himself—"at any rate, not old Dr. Burt's son.

"I used to come here to see your mother," said the doctor, "when she was sick. She used to talk a great deal about you, and said she wanted me to get acquainted with you, when your time was out."

Eph started, but said nothing.

"She was a good woman, Aunt Lois," added the doctor; "one of the best women I ever saw."

"I don't want anybody to bother himself on my account," said Eph. "I ask no favors."

"You will have to take favors, though," said the doctor, "before the winter is over. You will be careless and get sick; you have been living for a long time entirely in-doors, with regular hours and work and food. Now you are going to live out-of-doors, and get your own meals, irregularly. You did n't have on a thick coat the other night, when I saw you at the store."

"I haven't got any that's large enough for me," said Eph, a little less harshly, "and I 've got to keep my money for other things."

"Then look out and wear flannel shirts enough," said the doctor, "if you want to be independent. But before I go, I want to go into the house. I want my wife to see Aunt Lois's room, and the view from the west window;" and he led the way to the sleigh.

Eph hesitated a moment, and then followed him.

"Mary, this is Ephraim Morse. We are going in to see the Dutch tiles I have told you of."

She smiled as she held out her mittened hand to Eph, who took it awkwardly.

The square front room, which had been originally intended for a keeping-room, but had been Aunt Lois's bedroom, looked out from two windows upon the road, and from two upon the rolling, tumbling bay, and the shining sea beyond. A tall clock, with a rocking ship above the face, ticked in the corner. The painted floor with bright rag mats, the little table with a lacquer work-box, the stiff chairs and the old-fashioned bedstead, the china ornaments upon the mantel-piece, the picture of "The Emeline G. in the Harbor of Canton," were just as they had been when the patient invalid had lain there, looking from her pillow out to sea. In twelve rude tiles, set around the open fireplace, the Hebrews were seen in twelve stages of their escape from Egypt. It would appear from this representation that they had not restricted their borrowings to the jewels of their oppressors, but had taken for the journey certain Dutch clothing of the fashion of the seventeenth century. The scenery, too, was much like that about Leyden.

"I think," said the doctor's wife, "that the painter was just a little absent-minded when he put in that beer-barrel. And a wharf, by the Red Sea!"

"I wish you would conclude to rig your boat with a new sail," said the doctor, as he took up the reins, at parting. "There is n't a boat here that 's kept clean, and I should like to hire yours once or twice a week in summer, if you keep her as neat as you do your house. Come in and see me some evening, and we 'll talk it over."

Eph built his boat, and, in spite of his evident dislike of visitors, the inside finish and the arrangements of the little cabin were so ingenious and so novel that everybody had to pay him a visit.

True to his plan of being independent, he built in the side of the hill, near his barn, by a little gravelly pond, an ice-house, and with the hardest labor filled it, all by himself. With this supply, he would not have to go to the general wharf at Sandy Point to sell his fish, with the other men, but could pack and ship them himself. And he could do better, in this way, he thought, even after paying for teaming them to the cars.

The knowing ones laughed to see that, from asking no advice, he had miscalculated and laid in three times as much as he could use.

"Guess Eph cal'lates to fish with two lines in each hand an' another 'n his teeth," said Mr. Wing. "He 's plannin' out for a great lay o' fish."

The spring came slowly on, and the first boat that went out that season was Eph's. That day was one of unmixed delight to him. What a sense of absolute freedom, when he was fairly out beyond the lightship, with the fresh swiftness of the wind in his face! What an exquisite consciousness of power and control, as his boat went beating through the long waves! Two or three men from another village sailed across his wake. His boat lay over, almost showing her keel, now high out of water, now settling between the waves, while Eph stood easily in the stern, in his shirt-sleeves, backing against the tiller, smoking a pipe, and ranging the waters with his eyes.

"Takes it natural ag'in, don't he? Stands as easy as ef he was loafin' on a wharf," said one of the observers. "Expect it 's quite a treat to be out. But they do say he 's gittin' everybody's good opinion. They looked for a reg'-lar ruffi'n when he come home,—cuttin' nets, killin' cats, chasin' hens, gittin' drunk! They say Eliphalet Wood didn't hardly dare to go ou' doors for a month, 'thout havin' his hired man along. But he 's turned out as peaceful as a little gal."

One June day, as Eph was slitting blue-fish at the little pier which he had built on the bay shore, near his rude ice-house, two men came up.

"Hullo, Eph!"

"Hullo!"

"We 've got about sick, tradin' down to the wharf; we can't git no fair show. About one time in three, they tell us they don't want our fish, and won't take 'em unless we heave 'em in for next to nothin',—and we know there ain't no sense in it. So we just thought we 'd slip down and see 'f you would n't take 'em, seein's you 've got ice, and send 'em up with yourn."

Eph was taken all aback with this mark of confidence. The offer must be declined. It evidently sprang from some mere passing vexation.

"I can't buy fish," said he. "I have no scales to weigh 'em."

"Then send ourn in separate berrels," said one of the men.

"But I haven't any money to pay you," he said. "I only get my pay once a month."

"We'll git tick at William's, and you can settle 'th us when you git your pay."

"Well," said he, unable to refuse, "I 'll take 'em, if you say so."

Before the season was over, he had still another customer, and could have had three or four more, if he had had ice enough. He felt strongly inclined that fall to build a larger icehouse; and although he was a little afraid of bringing ridicule upon himself in case no fish should be brought to him the next summer, he decided to do so, on the assurance of three or four men that they meant to come to him. Nobody else had such a chance, — a pond right by the shore.

One evening there was a knock at the door of Eliphalet Wood, the owner of the burned barn. Eliphalet went to the door, but turned pale at seeing Eph there.

"Oh, come in, come in!" he panted. "Glad to see you. Walk in. Have a chair. Take a seat. Sit down."

But he thought his hour had come: he was alone in the house, and there was no neighbor within call.

Eph took out a roll of bills, counted out eighty dollars, laid the money on the table, and said quietly, —

"Give me a receipt on account."

When it was written he walked out, leaving Eliphalet stupefied.

Joshua Carr was at work, one June afternoon, by the roadside, in front of his low cottage, by an enormous pile of poles, which he was shaving down for barrel-hoops, when Eph appeared.

"Hard at it, Joshua!" he said.

"Yes, yes!" said Joshua, looking up through his steel-bowed spectacles. "Hev to work hard to make a livin'—though I don't know's I ought to call it hard, neither; and yet it is ruther hard, too; but then, on t' other hand, 't ain't so hard as a good many other things—though there is a good many jobs that's easier. That's so! that 's so!

> 'Must we be kerried to the skies
> On feathery beds of ease?'

Though I don't know's I ought to quote a hymn on such a matter; but then—I don' know's there's any partic'lar harm in't, neither."

Eph sat down on a pile of shavings and chewed a sliver; and the old man kept on at his work.

"Hoop-poles goin' up and hoops goin' down," he continued. "Cur'us, ain't it? But then, I don' know as 'tis; woods all bein' cut off—poles gittin' scurcer—hoops bein' shoved in from Down East. That don't seem just right, now, does it? But then, other folks must make a livin', too. Still, I should think they might take up suthin' else; and yet, they might say that about me. Understand, I don't mean to say that they actually do say so; I don't want to run down any man unless I know—"

"I can't stand this," said Eph to himself; "I don't wonder that they always used to put Joshua off at the first port, when he tried to go coasting. They said he talked them crazy with nothing.

"I 'll go into the house and see Aunt Lyddy," he said aloud. "I 'm loafing, this afternoon."

"All right! all right!" said Joshua. "Lyddy 'll be glad to see you—that is, as glad as she would be to see anybody," he added, reaching out for a pole. "Now, I don't s'pose that sounds very well; but still, you know how she is—she allers likes to hev folks to talk, and then she's allers sayin' talkin' wears on her; but I ought not to say that to you, because she allers likes to see you—that is, as much as she likes to see anybody. In fact, I think, on the whole—"

"Well, I'll take my chances," said Eph, laughing; and he opened the gate and went in.

Joshua's wife, whom everybody called Aunt Lyddy, was rocking in a high-backed-chair in the kitchen, and knitting. It was currently reported that Joshua's habit of endlessly retracting and qualifying every idea and modification of an idea which he advanced, so as to commit himself to nothing, was the effect of Aunt Lyddy's careful revision.

"I s'pose she thought 't was fun to be talked deef when they was courtin'," Captain Seth had once sagely remarked. "Prob'ly it sounded then like a putty piece on a seraphine; but I allers cal'lated she 'd git her fill of it, sooner or later. You most gin'lly git your fill o' one tune."

"How are you this afternoon, Aunt Lyddy?" asked Eph, walking in without knocking, and sitting down near her.

"So as to be able to keep about," she replied. "It is a great mercy I ain't afflicted with falling out of my chair, like Hepsy Jones, ain't it?"

"I 've brought you some oysters," he said. "I set the basket down on the door-step. I just took them out of the water myself from the bed I planted to the west of the water-fence."

"I always heard you was a great fisherman," said Aunt Lyddy, "but I had no idea you would ever come here and boast of being able to catch oysters. Poor things! How could they have got away? But why don't you bring them in? They won't be afraid of me, will they?"

He stepped to the door and brought in a peck basket full of large, black, twisted shells, and with a heavy clasp-knife proceeded to open one, and took out a great oyster, which he held up on the point of the blade.

"Try it," he said; and then Aunt Lyddy, after she had swallowed it, laughed to think what a tableau they had made,—a man who had been in the State prison standing over her with a great knife! And then she laughed again.

"What are you laughing at?" he said.

"It popped into my head, supposing Susan should have looked in at the south window and Joshua in at the door, when you was feeding out that oyster to me, what they would have thought!"

Eph laughed too; and, surely enough, just then a stout, light-haired, rather plain-looking young woman came up to the south window and leaned in. She had on a sun-bonnet, which had not prevented her from securing a few choice freckles. She had been working with a trowel in her flower-garden.

"What's the matter?" she said, nodding easily to Eph. "What do you two always find to laugh about?"

"Ephraim was feeding me with spoon-meat," said Aunt Lyddy, pointing to the basket, which looked like a basket of anthracite coal.

"It looks like spoon-meat!" said Susan, and then she laughed too. "I 'll roast some of them for supper," she added,—"a new way that I know."

Eph was not invited to stay to supper, but he stayed, none the less: that was always understood.

"Well, well, well!" said Joshua, coming to the door-step, and washing his hands and arms just outside, in a tin basin. "I thought I see you set down a parcel of oysters—but there was sea-weed over 'em, and I don' know's I could have said they was oysters; but then, if the square question had been put to me, 'Mr. Carr, be them oysters or be they not?' I s'pose I should have said they was; still, if they 'd asked me how I knew—"

"Come, come, father!" said Aunt Lyddy, "do give poor Ephraim a little peace. Why don't you just say you thought they were oysters, and done with it?"

"Say I *thought* they was?" he replied, innocently. "I knew well enough they was—that is—knew? No, I did n't know, but—"

Aunt Lyddy, with an air of mock resignation, gave up, while Joshua endeavored to fix, to a hair, the exact extent of his knowledge.

Eph smiled; but he remembered what would have made him pardon, a thousand times over, the old man's garrulousness. He remembered who alone had never failed, once a year, to visit a certain prisoner, at the cost of a long and tiresome journey, and who had written to that homesick prisoner kind and cheering letters, and had sent him baskets of simple dainties for holidays.

Susan bustled about, and made a fire of crackling sticks, and began to roast the oysters in a way that made a most savory smell. She set the table, and then sat down at the melodeon, while she was waiting, and sang a hymn; for she was of a musical turn, and was one of the choir. Then she jumped up and took out the steaming oysters, and they all sat down.

"Well, well, well!" said her father; "these be good! I did n't s'pose you hed any very good oysters in your bed, Ephraim. But there, now—I don't s'pose I ought to have said that; that was n't very polite; but what I meant was, I did n't s'pose you hed any that was *real* good—though I don' know but I 've said about the same thing, now. Well, any way, these be splendid; they 're full as good as those co-hogs we had t'other night."

"Quahaugs!" said Susan. "The idea of comparing these oysters with quahaugs!"

"Well, well! that's so!" said her father. "I did n't say right, did I, when I said that! Of course, there ain't no comparison—that is—*no* comparison? Why, of course, they is a comparison between everything,—but then, cohogs don't really compare with oysters! That's true!"

And then he paused to eat a few.

He was silent so long at this occupation that they all laughed.

"Well, well!" he said, laying down his fork, and smiling innocently; "what be you all laughin' at? Not but what I allers like to hev folks laugh—but then, I did n't see nothin' to laugh at. Still, perhaps they was suthin' to laugh at that I didn't see; sometimes one man 'll be lookin' down into his plate, all taken up with his victuals, and others, that's lookin' around the room, may see the kittens frolickin', or some such thing. 'T ain't the fust time I 've known all hands to laugh all to once-t, when I didn't see nothin'."

Susan helped him again, and secured another brief respite.

"Ephraim," said he, after a while, "you ain't skilled to cook oysters like this, I don't believe. You ought to git married! I was sayin' to Susan t'other day—well, now, mother, hev I said anything out o' the way? Well, I don't s'pose 't was just *my* place to have said anything about gitt'n' married, to Ephraim, seein's—"

"Come, come, father," said Aunt Lyddy, "that'll do, now. You must let Ephraim alone, and not joke him about such things."

Meanwhile Susan had hastily gone into the pantry to look for a pie, which she seemed unable at once to find.

"Pie got adrift?" called out Joshua. "Seems to me you don't hook on to it very quick. Now that looks good," he added, when she came out.

"That looks like cookin'! All I meant was, 't Ephraim ought not to be doin' his own cookin'—that is, 'f you can call it cookin. But then, of course, 'tis cookin'—there's all kinds o' cookin'. I went cook myself, when I was a boy."

After supper, Aunt Lyddy sat down to knit, and Joshua drew his chair up to an open window, to smoke his pipe. In this vice Aunt Lyddy encouraged him. The odor of Virginia tobacco was a sweet savor in her nostrils. No breezes from Araby ever awoke more grateful feelings than did the fragrance of Uncle Joshua's pipe. To Aunt Lyddy it meant quiet and peace.

Susan and Eph sat down on the broad flag door-stone, and talked quietly of the simple news of the neighborhood, and of the days when they used to go to school, and come home, always together.

"I did n't much think then," said Eph, "that I should ever bring up where I have, and get ashore before I was fairly out to sea!"

"Jehiel's schooner got ashore on the bar, years ago," said Susan, "and yet they towed her off, and I saw her this morning, from my chamber window, before sunrise, all sail set, going by to the eastward."

"I know what you mean," said Eph. "But here—I got mad once, and I almost had a right to, and I can't get started again; I never shall. I can get a living, of course; but I shall always be pointed out as a jailbird, and could no more get any footing in the world than Portuguese Jim."

Portuguese Jim was the sole professional criminal of the town,—a weak, good-natured, knock-kneed vagabond, who stole hens, and spent every winter in the House of Correction as an "idle and disorderly person."

Susan laughed outright at the picture. Eph smiled too, but a little bitterly.

"I suppose it was more ugliness than anything else," he said, "that made me come back here to live, where everybody knows I 've been in jail and is down on me."

"They are not down on you," said Susan. "Nobody is down on you. It 's all your own imagination. And if you had gone anywhere that you was a stranger, you know that the first thing that you would have done would have been to call a meeting and tell all the people that you had burned down a man's barn and been in the State's-prison, and that you wanted them all to know it at the start; and you wouldn't have told them why you did it, and how young you was then, and how Eliphalet treated your mother, and how you was going to pay him for all he lost Here, everybody knows that side of it. In fact," she added, with a little twinkle in her eye, "I have sometimes had an idea that the main thing they don't like is, to see you saving every cent to pay to Eliphalet."

"And yet it was on your say that I took up that plan," said Eph. "I never thought of it till you asked me when I was going to begin to pay him up."

"And you ought to," said Susan. "He has a right to the money—and then, you don't want to be under obligations to that man all your life. Now, what you want to do is to cheer up and go around among folks. Why, now you 're the only fish-buyer there is that the men don't watch when he 's weighing their fish. You'll own up to that, for one thing, won't you?"

"Well, they are good fellows that bring fish to me," he said.

"They were n't good fellows when they traded at the great wharf," said Susan. "They had a quarrel down there once a week, regularly."

"Well, suppose they do trust me in that," said Eph. "I can never rub out that I 've been in State's-prison."

"You don't want to rub it out. You can't rub anything out that's ever been; but you can do better than rub it out."

"What do you mean?"

"Take things just the way they are," said Susan, "and show what can be done. Perhaps you 'll stake a new channel out for others to follow in, that haven't half so much chance as you have. And that's what you will do, too," she added.

"Susan!" he said, "if there 's anything I can ever do, in this world or the next, for you or your folks, that's all I ask for,—the chance to do it. Your folks and you shall never want for anything while I'm alive.

"There's one thing sure," he added, rising. "I'll live by myself and be independent of everybody, and make my way all alone in the world; and if I can make 'em all finally own up and admit that I'm honest with 'em, I'm satisfied. That's all I 'll ever ask of anybody. But there's one thing that worries me sometimes,—that is, whether I ought to come here so often. I 'm afraid, sometimes, that it 'll hinder your father from gettin' work, or—something—for you folks to be friends with me."

"I think such things take care of themselves," said Susan, quietly. "If a chip won't float, let it sink."

"Good-night," said Eph; and he walked off, and went home to his echoing house.

After that, his visits to Joshua's became less frequent.

It was a bright day in March,—one of those which almost redeem the reputation of that desperado of a month. Eph was leaning on his fence, looking now down the bay and now to where the sun was sinking in the marshes. He knew that all the other men had gone to the town-meeting, where he had had no heart to intrude himself,— that free democratic parliament where he had often gone with his father in childhood; where the boys, rejoicing in a general assembly of their own, had played ball outside, while the men debated gravely within. He recalled the time when he himself had so proudly given his first vote for President, and how his father had introduced him then to friends from distant parts of the town. He remembered how he had heard his father speak there, and how respectfully everybody had listened to him. That was in the long ago, when they had lived at the great farm. And then came the thought of the mortgage, and of Eliphalet's foreclosure, and—

"Hullo, Eph!"

It was one of the men from whom he took fish,—a plain-spoken, sincere little man.

"Why wa'n't you down to town-meet'n'?"

"I was busy," said Eph.

"How'd ye like the news?"

"What news?"

There was never any good news for him now.

"Hain't heard who 's elected town-clerk?"

"No."

Had they elected Eliphalet, and so expressed their settled distrust of him, and sympathy for the man whom he had injured?

"Who is elected?" he asked harshly.

"You be!" said the man; "went in flyin',—all hands clappin' and stompin' their feet!"

An hour later the doctor drove up, stopped, and walked toward the kitchen door. As he passed the window, he looked in.

Eph was lying on his face, upon the settle, as he had first seen him there, his arms beneath his head.

"I will not disturb him now," said the doctor.

One breezy afternoon, in the following summer, Captain Seth laid aside his easy every-day clothes, and transformed himself into a stiff broadcloth image, with a small silk hat and creaking boots. So attired, he set out in a high open buggy, with his wife, also in black, but with gold spectacles, to the funeral of an aunt. As they pursued their jog-trot journey along the Salt Hay Road, and came to Ephraim Morse's cottage, they saw Susan sitting in a shady little porch at the front door, shelling peas and looking down the bay.

"How is everything, Susan?" called out Captain Seth; "'bout time for Eph to be gitt'n' in?"

"Yes," she answered, nodding and smiling, and pointing with a pea-pod; "that's our boat, just coming to the wharf, with her peak down."

Lightning Source UK Ltd.
Milton Keynes UK
UKHW010633140621
385483UK00001B/103